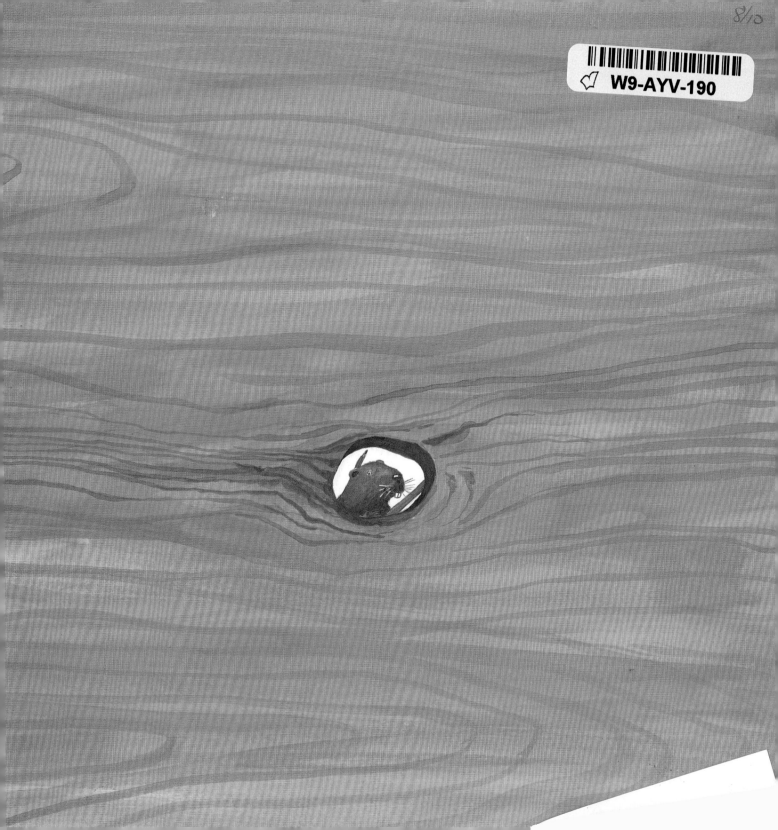

Henry Holt and Company, Inc.
Publishers since 1866
115 West 18th Street
New York, New York 10011

Henry Holt is a registered trademark of Henry Holt and Company, Inc.

Copyright © 1995 by Lars Klinting
Translation copyright © 1996 by Henry Holt and Company, Inc.
First published in the United States in 1996 by Henry Holt and Company, Inc.
Originally published in Sweden in 1995 by
Alfabeta Bokförlag AB under the title
Castor Snickrar.

Library of Congress Cataloging-in-Publication Data
Klinting, Lars. [Castor snickrar. English]
  Bruno the carpenter / by Lars Klinting.
  Summary: Bruno the beaver, a carpenter, studies his
plans carefully and then builds a toolbox step by step.
  [1. Carpenters—Fiction. 2. Beavers—Fiction.] I. Title.
PZ7.K682Br 1996 [E]—dc20 95-23398

ISBN 0-8050-4501-5
First American Edition—1996
Printed in China Polex Intl. AB 1995
10 9 8 7 6 5 4 3 2 1

The artist used watercolors and colored
pencil to create the illustrations for this book.

LARS KLINTING

BRUNO
the Carpenter

HENRY HOLT AND COMPANY

NEW YORK

Aha! Here are the plans he was looking for.
Now his work can begin.

This is Bruno's workshop. Bruno's grandfather built the
carpenter's table. It is very old. Bruno built the green stool.
It is brand-new.

Bruno's workshop is messy. He has trouble finding what he
needs. He's looking for something right now.

This is Bruno the carpenter.

He studies the plans carefully, so he won't make any mistakes.

Then he takes out

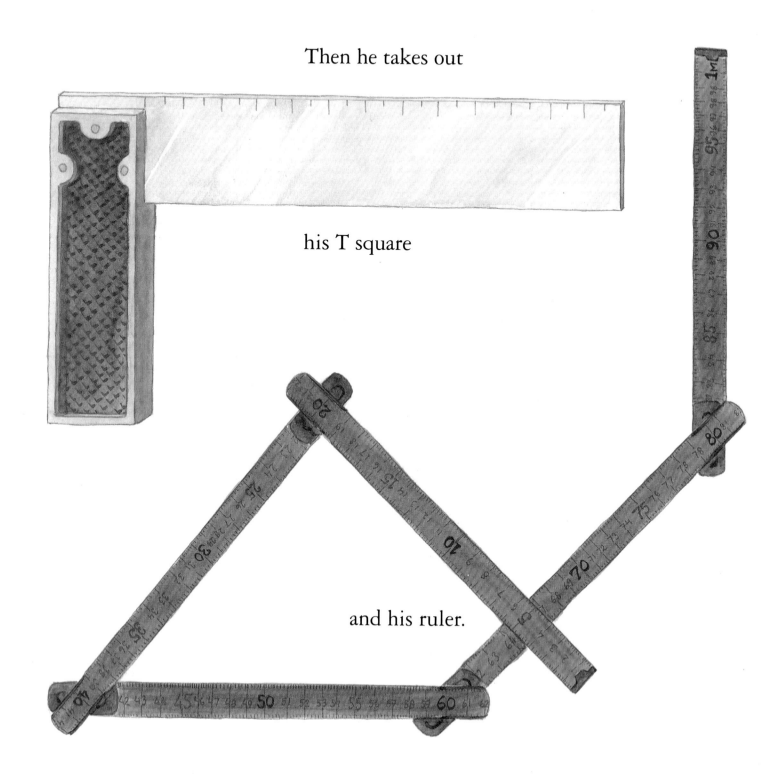

his T square

and his ruler.

Bruno measures the wood with his ruler. He marks it with a pencil so he'll know where to saw and drill.

Some lines are curved, and some lines are straight. The T square helps him with the straight lines.

Then Bruno takes out

his crosscut saw.

He saws the wood on the straight lines he marked with his pencil.

Next he takes out

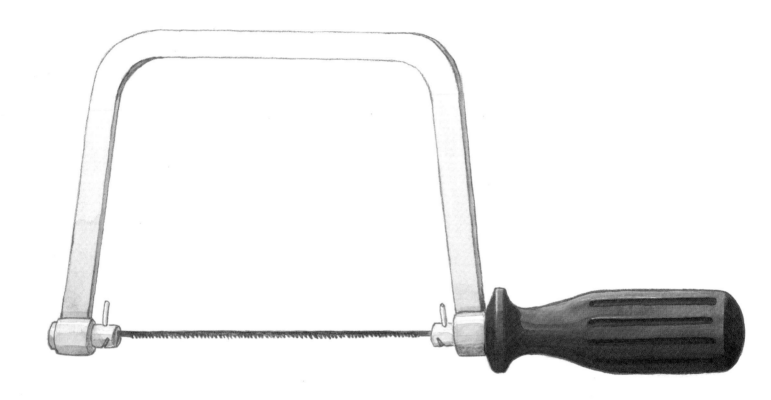

his jigsaw.

He uses it to saw the rounded shapes.

Now Bruno wants to
drill some big holes.

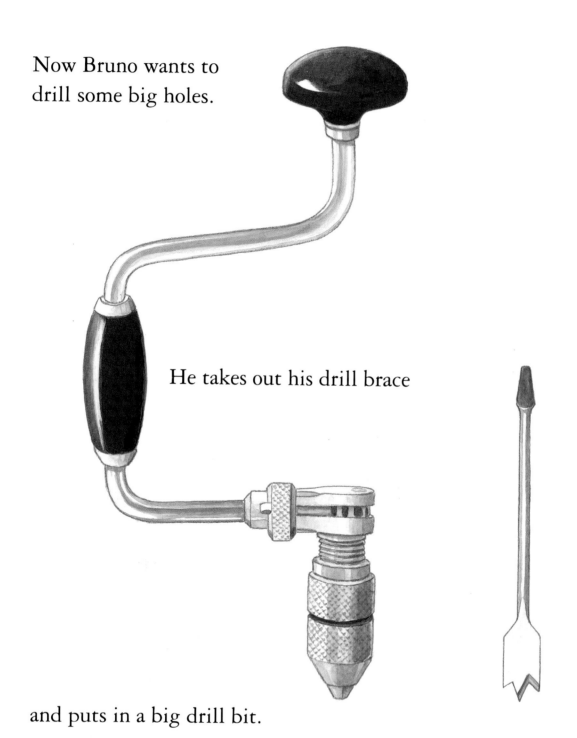

He takes out his drill brace

and puts in a big drill bit.

His stool comes in handy for drilling the big holes.

Next Bruno wants to
drill some small holes.

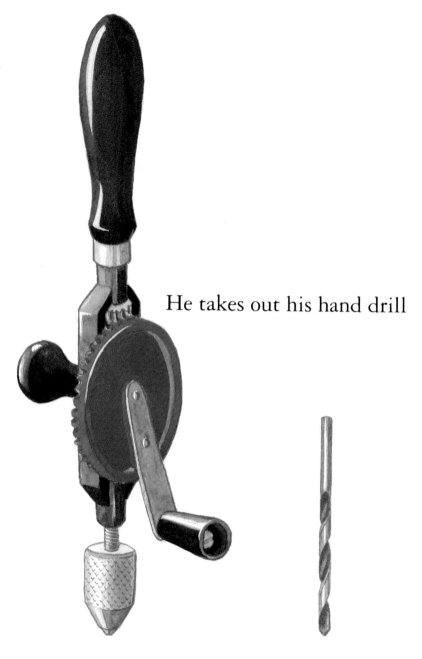

He takes out his hand drill

and puts in a small drill bit.

His stool comes in handy for drilling the small holes, too.

Now all the pieces of wood have to be smoothed and polished. Bruno doesn't want splinters in his fingers.

He takes out a file

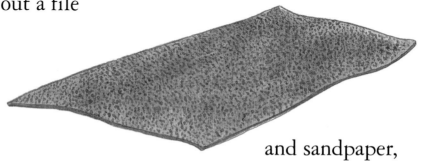

and sandpaper,

which he wraps around a sanding block.

First he files the edges of each piece. Then he polishes them with his sandpaper until they are smooth.

Now it's time to put all the pieces together.
First he takes out

a screwdriver

and a box of screws.

The screws fit in the small holes.

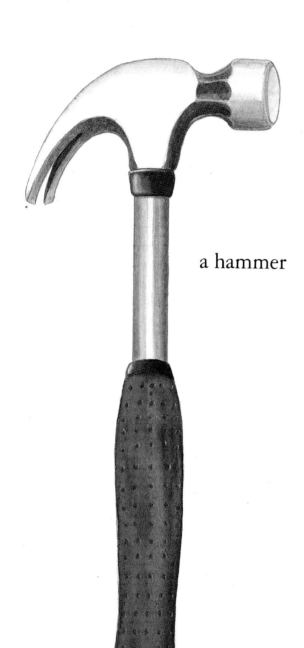

a hammer

Then he takes out

and a box of nails.

Ooops! He bent the nail!

Bruno has to get

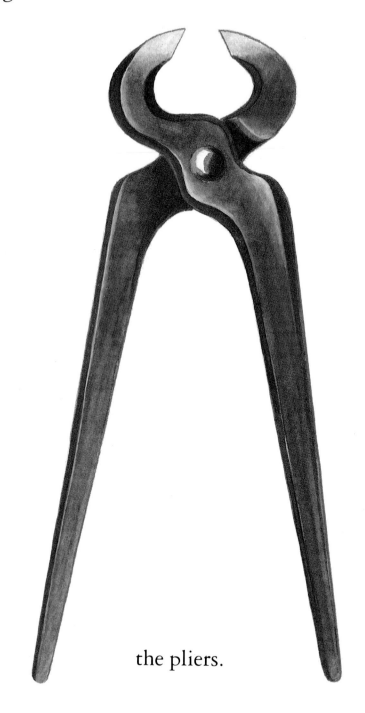

the pliers.

He pulls out the crooked nail and hammers in a new one.

Bruno's work is almost finished. But he still needs

a mallet   and some glue.

He taps in the last piece. It fits in the large holes.

Finally, Bruno takes out all his tools:

the crosscut saw

the file

the nails

the jigsaw

the screws

the sandpaper and sanding block

the pliers

the hammer

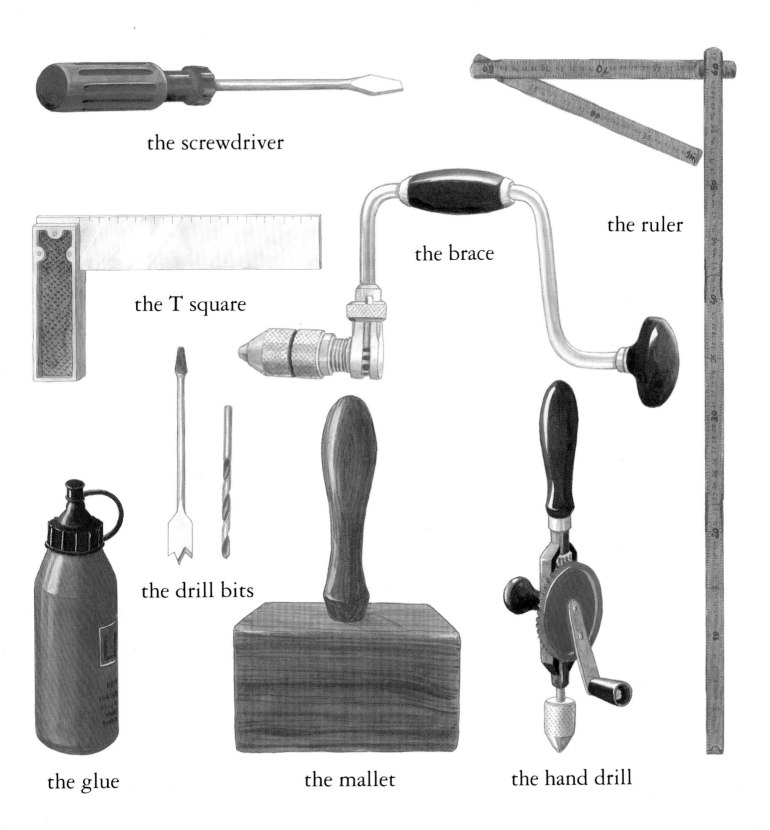

the screwdriver

the ruler

the T square

the brace

the drill bits

the glue

the mallet

the hand drill

. . . and he puts them in his new toolbox.

Bruno's Toolbox Plans

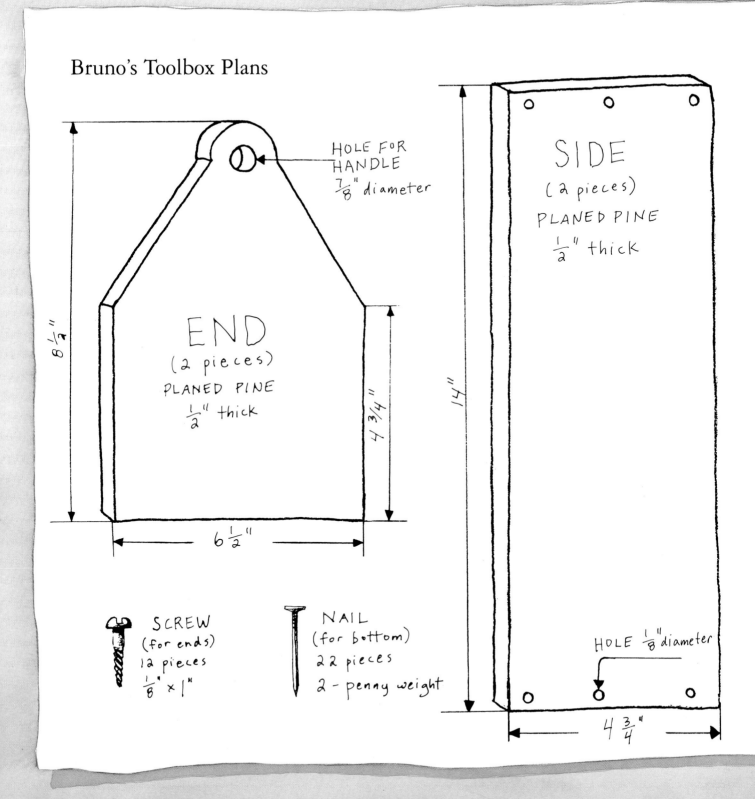

HOLE FOR HANDLE $\frac{7}{8}$" diameter

END
(2 pieces)
PLANED PINE
$\frac{1}{2}$" thick

$8\frac{1}{2}$"

$4\frac{3}{4}$"

$6\frac{1}{2}$"

SIDE
(2 pieces)
PLANED PINE
$\frac{1}{2}$" thick

14"

SCREW
(for ends)
12 pieces
$\frac{1}{8}$" x 1"

NAIL
(for bottom)
22 pieces
2 - penny weight

HOLE $\frac{1}{8}$" diameter

$4\frac{3}{4}$"

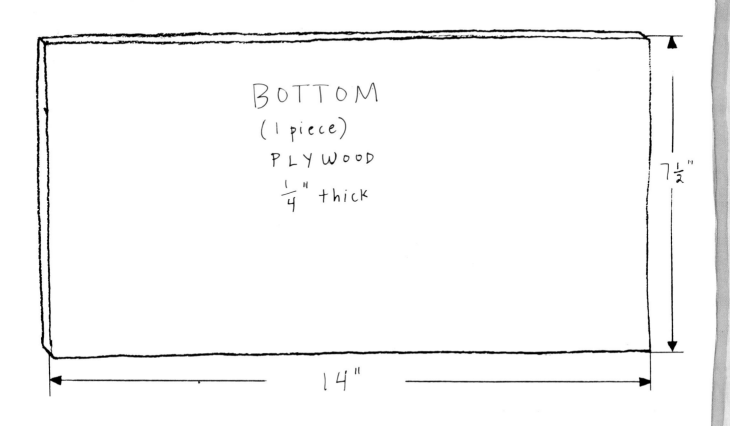

BOTTOM
(1 piece)
PLYWOOD
$\frac{1}{4}$" thick

$7\frac{1}{2}$"

14"

GLUE INTO END

GLUE INTO END

HANDLE $\frac{7}{8}$" dowel

14"